MAGIC DOOR TO LEARNING

One Summery Day

Written by Larry Dane Brimner • Illustrated by R. W. Alley

Published in the United States of America by The Child's World®
PO Box 326 • Chanhassen, MN 55317-0326
800-599-READ • www.childsworld.com

Reading Adviser

Cecilia Minden-Cupp, PhD, Director of Language and Literacy, Harvard University Graduate School of Education, Cambridge, Massachusetts

Acknowledgments

The Child's World®: Mary Berendes, Publishing Director

Editorial Directions, Inc.: E. Russell Primm, Editorial Director and Project Manager; Katie Marsico, Associate Editor; Judith Shiffer, Assistant Editor; Matt Messbarger, Editorial Assistant

The Design Lab: Kathleen Petelinsek, Design and art production

Library of Congress Cataloging-in-Publication Data

Brimner, Larry Dane.
  One summery day / written by Larry Dane Brimner ; illustrated by R. W. Alley.
    p. cm. – (Magic door to learning)
  Summary: A child describes some of the sights and sounds of summer.
  ISBN 1-59296-518-0 (lib. bdg. : alk. paper) [1. Summer—Fiction.] I. Alley, R. W. (Robert W.),
ill. II. Title.
  PZ7.B767On 2005
  [E]—dc22   2005005362

A book is a door, a magic door.
It can take you places
you have never been before.
Ready? Set?
Turn the page.
Open the door.
Now it is time to explore.

Summer is sleeping
late because there
is no school and

swinging in the
cool shade of
the walnut tree.

Summer is a good
book and a pitcher of
lemonade on the porch.

Sometimes summer is a day at the shore!

My little brother and
I pile out of the car.
We race across the
hot sand, our fins
flipping and flopping.

We jump over waves until
we can jump no more.

Then we duck under the water.

Later, we fill our buckets and
try to sneak up on Mom.

She sees us and cries out,
"Oh, no! Sea monsters!"
We slosh water on her.

And she chases us back
down to the shore,
back into the water.
We splash and giggle
and giggle and splash.

Mom makes us seaweed necklaces.

19

We search for seashells.

My little brother fills his bucket full!

Before we go, we build a sandcastle
with three tall towers and a moat

on one summery day at the shore.

Our story is over, but there is still much to explore beyond the magic door!

Have you ever hunted for seashells? The next time you're at the beach, see how many shells you can collect. Try to gather many different kinds. Ask an adult to help you figure out what kind of animal used to live inside.

These books will help you explore at the library and at home:

Parr, Todd. *Otto Goes to the Beach.* Boston: Little, Brown, 2003.

Roosa, Karen, and Maggie Smith (illustrator). *Beach Day.* New York: Clarion Books, 2001.

About the Author

Larry Dane Brimner is an award-winning author of more than 120 books for children. When he isn't at his computer writing, he can be found biking in Colorado or hiking in Arizona. You can visit him online at *www.brimner.com.*

About the Illustrator

R. W. Alley has illustrated more than seventy-five books for children and has authored five of these. Since 1997, he has served as the illustrator on Michael Bond's Paddington Bear series. Alley lives in Barrington, Rhode Island, with his wife and two children. He often visits local elementary schools to discuss how words and pictures come together to form books.